THE GiRL WHO NEVER MADE MiSTAKES

by MARK PETT and GARY RUBINSTEIN

ILLUSTRATED by MARK PETT

sourcebooks
jabberwocky

For Millie and Sarah

Published by Sourcebooks Jabberwocky, an imprint of Sourcebooks, Inc.
P.O. Box 4410, Naperville, Illinois 60567-4410
(630) 961-3900
Fax: (630) 961-2168
www.jabberwockykids.com

Library of Congress Cataloging-in-Publication data is on file with the publisher.

Source of Production: Leo Paper, Heshan City, Guangdong Province, China
Date of Production: August 2011
Run Number: 15429

Printed and bound in China.
LEO 10 9 8 7 6 5 4 3 2 1

For Beatrice Bottomwell,
Friday began like any other day.

She matched her socks. And, of course,
she put her shoes on their proper feet.

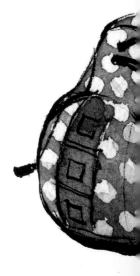

She remembered to feed her hamster, Humbert, his favorite food, broccoli.

And when she made a sandwich for her brother Carl's lunch, she used exactly the same amount of peanut butter as jelly.

When she stepped outside to greet her fans, she didn't forget to say "good morning" and "thank you."

They asked if she made her bed. She had.

They asked if she forgot to do her math homework. Nope.

"What about tonight's talent show?" they asked. "I'm ready!" said Beatrice with a smile. After all, her juggling act had won three years in a row.

Most people in town didn't even know Beatrice's name.

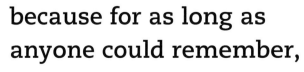

They just called her "the Girl Who Never Makes Mistakes,"

because for as long as anyone could remember,

she never did.

Unlike Beatrice, Carl
made lots of mistakes.

He ate his crayons
and drew with his
green beans.

He danced with his hands
and played the piano with
his feet.

Carl loved to make mistakes!

At school, Beatrice was on a cooking team with her two best friends, Millie and Sarah. To make their giant rhubarb muffins, they needed four eggs.

Beatrice went to the refrigerator and carefully chose the biggest, eggiest eggs she could find.

But on the way back, her legs slipped out from under her.

The eggs went flying.

Beatrice was about to make her first mistake...

For the rest of the school day, Beatrice could not stop thinking about her Almost Mistake.

On her way home from school, Beatrice watched Millie and Sarah ice-skating in the park.

"Come join us!" said Millie. "It's fun!" said Sarah.

Beatrice watched them slip and slide on the frozen pond. Millie and Sarah laughed as they wobbled on the ice.

"No, thanks," said Beatrice.

At supper, Beatrice barely touched her food.

"Is everything all right, kiddo?" asked her father.

"I'm worried I'll mess up tonight," said Beatrice. "And everyone will be watching."

"Worry? You don't make mistakes!" he said with a smile.

Beatrice tried to smile too.

After supper, Beatrice got ready for the talent show.

First, she woke Humbert from his nap.

Next, she got the salt shaker from the kitchen table.

Finally, she filled a balloon with water.

The school auditorium was packed! Beatrice felt her stomach jumping around inside her.

Beatrice waited for her juggling music to begin.

"That's her! That's the Girl Who Never Makes Mistakes!" said a woman.

"Oh! We know she'll be perfect!" said a man.

When the music started, she tossed Humbert into the air.

Next, she added the salt shaker.

And finally, the water balloon.

Beatrice didn't miss a beat! The crowd clapped with delight.

But Beatrice noticed something odd about the salt shaker...

The specks falling out of it were not white!

AAHHCH

Humbert, pieces of water balloon, and the pepper rained down on top of Beatrice.

For the first time in as long as anyone could remember, Beatrice made a mistake.

And it was a big one!

The music stopped.

Beatrice didn't know
what to do.

Cry?

Run off the stage?

The crowd sat stunned.
They couldn't believe that
the Girl Who Never Makes
Mistakes made a mistake!

Beatrice looked up at Humbert.

He looked back at her.

His hamster fur was soaked and speckled with bits of balloon.

Beatrice let out a giggle.
The giggle grew into a chuckle.
And the chuckle became a laugh.

The people in the crowd looked at each other and then back at Beatrice. They began to giggle. Then chuckle. Then—finally—roar with laughter.

Beatrice and the audience laughed until they couldn't remember why they were laughing.

That night, Beatrice
slept better than
she ever had!

In the morning, no fans greeted Beatrice.

When she got dressed, Beatrice—for no reason at all—put a polka dot sock on one foot and a plaid sock on the other.

Beatrice and Carl made sandwiches. This time, they put the peanut butter and jelly on the outside. They called it an Inside Out PB & J!

Lunch was messy and delicious!

Later, Beatrice found Millie and
Sarah skating in the park.

They fell a lot. And laughed!

Now, people no longer call her the Girl Who Never Makes Mistakes.

They just call her Beatrice.